Percy Police
Percy saves the day

Pamela Malcolm

Percy Police Car

By Pamela Malcolm

Thank you to the Emergency Services for your hard work keeping us safe.

If you enjoy this book I would love it if you could leave me feedback.

Please also visit my author page to get more books in the Ruby & Billy series.

Percy Police Car is getting ready for a well-deserved afternoon nap. It has been so busy in Carville the past few weeks and he really needs to get some rest. Just as he is about to doze-off officers York and Diaz come out of the station. Officer York always looks like she just woke up from a five day nap. Percy Police Car has never even seen Officer Diaz eat or sleep, it's like he is robot!

"No time for napping!" officer Diaz said. "Sorry, Percy, we know you've been working really hard lately, but our shift is about to start!" Officer York says softly. Percy Police Car admires the two officers. They are never too tired or too busy to help the citizens of Carville. He blinks his eyes and fires up his engine, "Let's go!" Percy says, ready to save the day!

Percy Police Car and the two officers start by driving down Main Street. People slow down when they see him driving down the street, Percy finds this funny. People wave at Percy as he passes and children point at him while saying, "Look, there's Percy the brave Police Car!" Sometimes he feels like a celebrity.

They park on the corner of Ford Street and Chevy Lane. They keep their eyes peeled for cars driving too fast or dangerously. Percy knows that it's his duty to find anyone who is doing something wrong in Carville. Locking up the baddies, keep Carville's citizens safe.

After five minutes Percy gets a call over his radio. "A big truck has broken down on the highway and is blocking traffic. We need all police officers in the area to report to the scene, now!" the voice says. Officer Diaz replies, "Copy that! We are on our way!"

"Looks like the day is starting early," Officer York says, "Are you ready, Percy?"

"I'm always ready!" Percy replies excited.
Percy puts on his siren and lights. He revs his engine and
speeds to the scene. Cars give way when they see the
police lights and hear the loud siren so that Percy, Officer
Diaz and Officer York could pass by quickly. People know
that they are heading to an emergency. "Go save the day,
Percy!" someone yells from their car.

They reach the scene where the truck has broken down because of a burst wheel. The driver looks very upset but is not hurt. The traffic is really bad. A queue of cars is building up, waiting to pass the truck.

"Percy! Percy!" he hears someone calling his name. It's Penny, Percy's fellow police car! He says hello by honking his horn.

"Whoa! You got here pretty quickly?" Percy asks Penny.

"We were only a mile away," Penny replied, "chasing some baddies who robbed Mr. Smith's Jewellery Story!"

"Did you catch them?" Percy asked. "Of course we did!" Penny answered with a playful smile when they hear a loud fire truck siren coming from the queue.
Penny and Percy spot Fiona Fire Truck stuck in the traffic. She looks very worried and in a hurry. Fiona's lights and siren are on but people aren't moving out of the way. "She must be trying to get to a fire!" Percy cries.

"We need to help her!" Penny says. They jump into action and both put on their lights again. They drive along the traffic, getting people to move over. The officers wave with their arms asking people to make way. They make a clear path for Fiona and she can finally get through! Fiona honks a "Thank you!" to Percy and Penny as she speeds by.

Their work is far from done. More cars have joined the queue and people are honking impatiently. "What's taking so long?" "What's going on there?" and "Why are we stuck?" are some of the questions being yelled from the cars. The officers in Penny Police Car calm the people down by answering questions and reassuring them that everything is under control.

Officers Diaz and York get out of the police car and start to direct traffic around the truck. Cars are slowly moving and the queue is getting shorter by the minute. As the cars drive pass the truck they thank the police officers with smiles.

After a few minutes Percy spots a tow truck trying to get through. He guides the tow truck towards the broken down vehicle. Some men offer to help the tow truck and soon enough the broken down vehicle has been moved out of the way.

Soon time all the traffic is gone and the cars can safely reach their destinations. The truck driver looks relieved and thanks Percy and the officers for their help, "Thank you so much for saving me today!"
"It's our pleasure and duty," Percy replies.

"Another problem solved," Officer York says and gives Percy Police Car a high five on his side mirror. At that moment a call comes from Percy's radio, "

A robbery on the corner of Chevy Lane and Ferrari Street, the robber is on foot and escaping, we need all nearby police officers to report to the surrounding scene!"
"Shift's not over yet," Officer Diaz says.
"I'm ready to go!" Percy Police Car replies.

Percy wonders what else will happen today, being a Police Car can be very dangerous but also very exciting. He will surely be ready for that nap later.

Thank you for reading........

Please remember to leave a review if you enjoyed my book it would be nice to hear what you and your children thought of this book☺

Thank you for your time.

Pamela

If you enjoyed this book please also check out these books in the Billy, Ruby and Emergency Services Series below.......

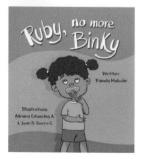

Please visit Aryla Publishing for more books by Pamela Malcolm and other great Authors. Sign up to be informed of upcoming free book promotions and a chance to win prizes in our monthly prize draw.

Please visit Aryla Publishing
and Follow us on Facebook Instagram & Twitter
Thank you for your support!

**Other children series published by
Aryla Publishing**
Author Casey L Adams
Body Goo 1 Sneezing
Body Goo 2 Burping
Body Goo 3 Farting
Body Goo 4 Vomiting
Body Goo 5 The Crusty Bits
Body Goo 6 The Sticky Bits
Love Bugs Don't Step on The Ant
Love Bugs Don't Splat The Spider

Coming Soon.........

- *Billy's Wobbly Tooth*

Visit www.arylapublishing.com to find out about all new releases.

Also Subscribe to Billy's Monthly Vlog on Youtube to find out what he is up to.

New Vlogs every month

Printed in Great Britain
by Amazon

73538117R00015